This Little Tiger
book belongs to:

_____

_____

_____

For Helen, with my love ~ P B

To illustration ~ M T

LITTLE TIGER PRESS
An imprint of Magi Publications
1 The Coda Centre, 189 Munster Road, London SW6 6AW
www.littletigerpress.com

First published in Great Britain 2009
This edition published 2009
Text copyright © Paul Bright 2009
Illustrations copyright © Michael Terry 2009
Paul Bright and Michael Terry have asserted their rights
to be identified as the author and illustrator of this work
under the Copyright, Designs and Patents Act, 1988
All rights reserved
ISBN 978-1-84506-987-2
A CIP catalogue record for this book
is available from the British Library
Printed in China
2 4 6 8 10 9 7 5 3 1

CRUNCH MUNCH
DINOSAUR LUNCH!

Paul Bright   Michael Terry

LITTLE TIGER PRESS
London

Ty was big, and Ty was mean. He had a big, big mouth, with big, big jaws, and big, big teeth and big, big, claws.

"Yeah! That's me," said Ty tyrannosaurus.

His roar echoed around the swamp,
so that the other dinosaurs trembled
in their tummies.

ROAR!

Teri was small and Teri was sweet. She had a tiny, tiny mouth, with tiny, tiny jaws, and tiny, tiny teeth and tiny, tiny claws. And she loved her big brother more than any tyrannosaurus has ever been loved.

"Lub oo, Ty rannynormus!"

gurgled Teri.

"Stay in your nest, pest," said Ty.

"I've got hunting to do."

Ty stomped through the swamp.
The ground sploshed and quaked and
quivered, and the dinosaurs heard,
and shook and shivered.

"I'M HUNGRY!" roared Ty.

"I'M BIGGEST, I'M BADDEST,
I'M READY TO EAT.
I NEED SOME FRESH
STEGOSAURUS MEAT!"

He opened his big, big mouth and . . .

"Hug oo, Ty rannynormus!"
burbled Teri, wrapping her
arms around his huge leg.

Ty sighed as he saw his stegosaurus breakfast
paddle off through the swamp, sniggering.
"You shouldn't be here, squirt!" he hissed.
"Get back to your drooling. Now stay away!"
And off he stomped, snorting.

Ty searched in the swamp. The dinosaurs ran and hid. They peered through the reeds and peeked from behind rocks. But it's not easy to hide when you're a dinosaur.

"I'M STARVING!" roared Ty.

"I'M BIGGEST, I'M BADDEST,
I'M READY FOR LUNCH!
I NEED TRICERATOPS
BONES TO CRUNCH!"

He bared his big, big teeth and . . .

"Kiss oo, Ty rannynormus!" slobbered Teri, planting a wet, sloppy kiss on his huge cheek.

Ty moaned as he saw his triceratops lunch plodding through the trees, laughing.

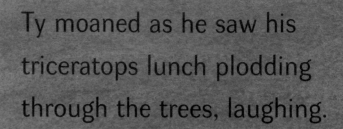

"You crawling, bawling bug!" he growled.
"Get back to your slurping and burping.
Now leave me alone!" And off he
stormed, snarling.

Ty crept through the swamp, quiet as quiet.
The other dinosaurs stayed still as still,
and even the leaves stopped rustling.
But a dinosaur can't stay still for long.
Ty heard a movement in the trees
and saw a long, long neck.

"I AM RAVENOUS!" roared Ty.
"I'M BIGGEST, I'M BADDEST,
I'M READY FOR TEA!
DIPLODOCUS STEAK LOOKS
TASTY TO ME!"

He roared a big, big roar and . . .

"Cuggle oo, Ty rannynormus!"
cooed Teri.

Ty groaned as his
diplodocus tea waddled
into the reed bed, chuckling.

"You spoiling, sniffling, dribbling, burbling, gurgling pest!" he bellowed. "I've had nothing to eat all day because of you.

"GRRRR!
I'M GOING HOME!"

Ty stomped off through the swamp, then pounded
across the plain in a great temper. Teri watched
him getting further and further away. Then
she sat down in a heap, and howled.

THUD! THUD! THUD!

Suddenly . . . the ground trembled.
"Ty rannynormus!" squeaked Teri.

But it wasn't.

IT WAS SPINOSAURUS!

Teri screamed. Spinosaurus was huge –
bigger even than her big brother Ty.
He had a huge, huge mouth, with
huge, huge teeth, and his
mouth was opening
wider and wider!

"DON'T YOU TOUCH
MY BABY SISTER!"

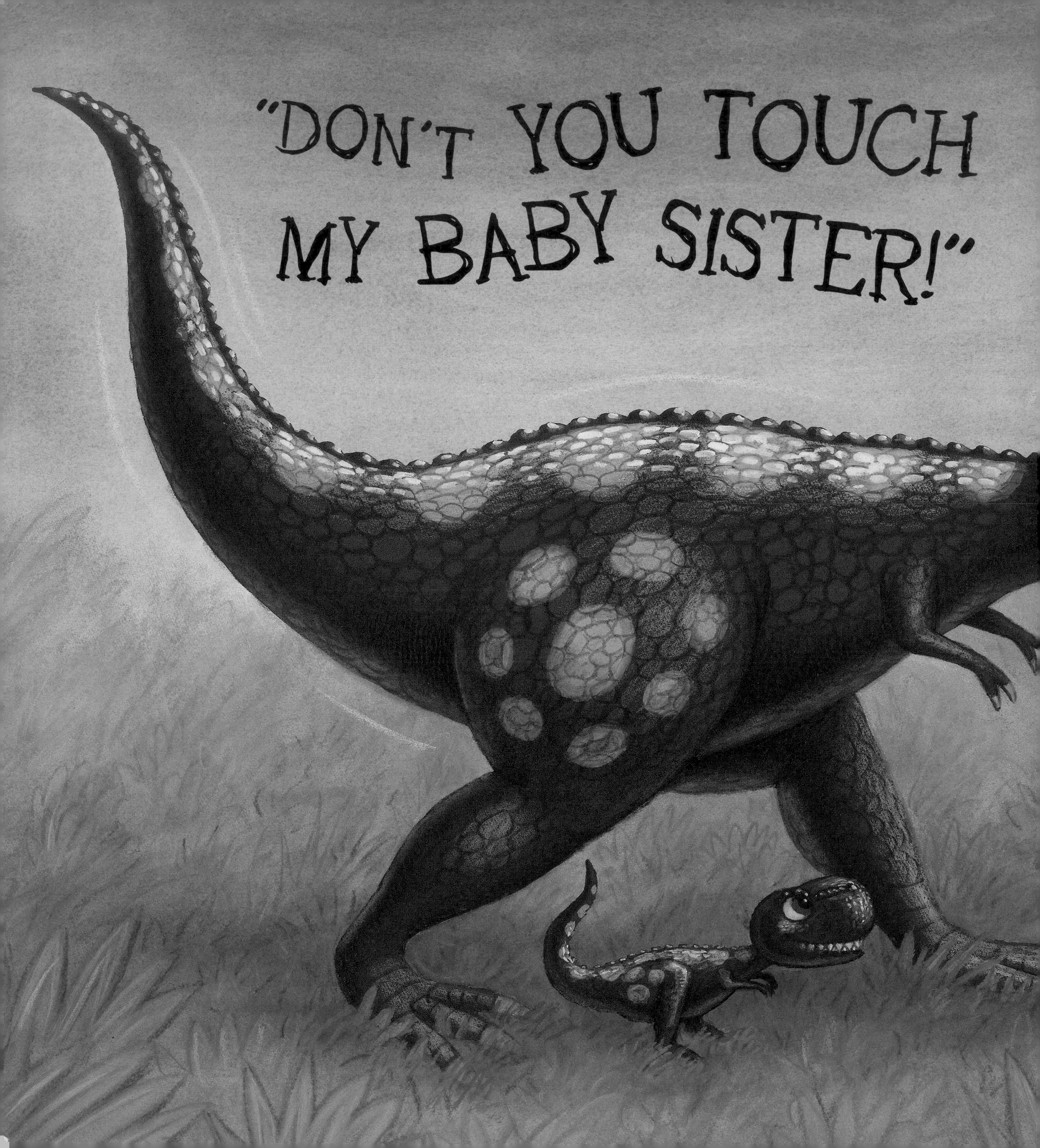

Ty roared and raged. He charged and chased.
And Spinosaurus turned and ran,
as fast as his lumbering
legs could go.

Then Ty reached down and scooped up Teri in his big, brotherly arms. He hugged his favourite, very annoying pest of a sister more tightly than any tyrannosaurus has ever been hugged.

"Lub oo, Ty rannynormus,"

gurgled Teri.

"Lub oo too, Teri rannynormus,"

said Ty, with a big, big smile.

"Now let's go get some dinner!"